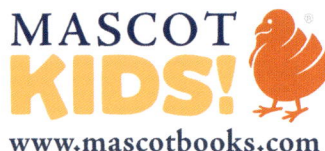

www.mascotbooks.com

Honey's Lost Shoe

©2022 Shar'Bral Jones. All Rights Reserved. No part of this publication may be reproduced, stored in a retrieval system or transmitted in any form by any means electronic, mechanical, or photocopying, recording or otherwise without the permission of the author.

For more information, please contact:
Mascot Books
620 Herndon Parkway #320
Herndon, VA 20170
info@mascotbooks.com

CPSIA Code: PRT0821A
Library of Congress Control Number: 2020912102
ISBN-13: 978-1-64543-589-1

Printed in the United States of America

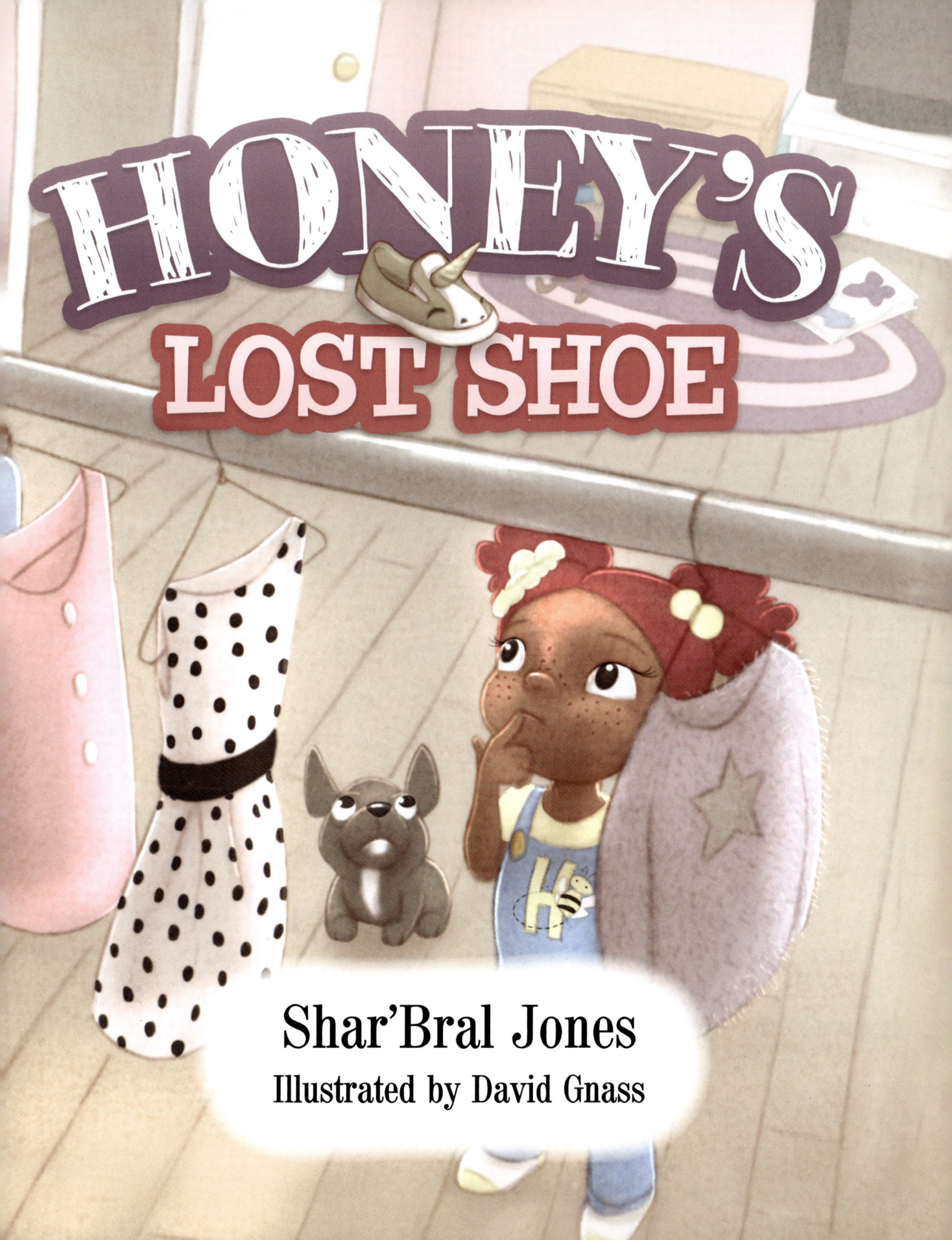

To my fiancé, family, and friends for always supporting my dreams and believing in me.

To my son, Zaylen–this is what Mommy was doing while you were in my tummy. I love you!

For every child who loves to read and has been on a scavenger hunt for a lost shoe or favorite toy–thank YOU!

It was a nice sunny day, and Honey wanted to play. She went to her closet to look for her shoes.

Honey only found one. What will she do? "I know," said Honey. "I'll search HIGH and low."

Honey started her search in the kitchen. "Let's see, if I were a shoe, where would I go missing?"

Honey looked **above** the counter, but all that was there was a shiny, red apple.

"No shoe up here," said Honey. "Oh, where could it be? I'll check the living room. I bet it's there. You'll see!"

In the living room, Honey looked **beside** the sofa. "No shoe here!" said Honey. "Just a **green** crayon."

Honey looked above the counter and beside the sofa, but her shoe wasn't there. "Oh, where could it be? I'll check the dining room. I bet it's there. You'll see!"

In the dining room, Honey looked **in front of** the bookshelf. "No shoe here," said Honey. "Just an orange barrette."

Honey looked above the counter, beside the sofa, and in front of the bookshelf. "Oh, where could it be? I'll check the bathroom. I bet it's there. You'll see!"

Honey walked into the bathroom. "Let's see, if I were a shoe, where would I be?" Honey looked **inside** the tub. "No shoe here," said Honey. "Just a yellow rubber duckie."

Honey looked above the counter, beside the sofa, in front of the bookshelf, and inside the tub. "Oh, where could it be? I'll check Mom's bedroom. I bet it's there. You'll see."

In Mom's bedroom there were so many things. "This is really beginning to wreck my brain." Honey looked **below** the window. "No shoe here," said Honey. "Just a blue bracelet."

Honey looked above the counter, beside the sofa, in front of the bookshelf, inside the tub, and below the window. "Oh, where could it be? I'll check my room! I bet it's there. You'll see!"

In her bedroom, Honey thought, *This is not right! This is just mean!* She looked at her TV and her toy chest, and then she looked **in between**. "No shoe here," said Honey. "Just a **purple** sock."

Honey looked above the counter, beside the sofa, in front of the bookshelf, inside the tub, below the window, and in between the toy chest and the TV. "Oh, where could it be? I'll check under my bed. I bet it's there. You'll see."

Under her bed, Honey looked to the left and then to the right. "No shoe here," said Honey. "Just one shiny, **brown** penny."

Honey looked above the counter, beside the sofa, in front of the bookshelf, inside the tub, below the window, in between the toy chest and the TV, and under her bed. "Oh, where could it be?"

Honey was out of ideas for where to look.
She sat on her bed and began to read a book.

Mom entered the room with a smile on her face.
"Honey the Shoe Detective, did you solve the case?"

Honey looked up, and on her face a frown appeared.
"No, Mom, it must've disappeared."

"I'm sorry, Honey. Don't give up," said Mom.
She left the room and closed the door.
"My shoe!" shouted Honey. It was **behind** it on the floor.

"Silly shoe!" said Honey. "So this is where you've been? Now, where is my sweater?"

Here we go again!

About the Author

Shar'Bral Jones teaches second grade in Philadelphia, Pennsylvania, and absolutely loves her job! Shar'Bral won the Constance Clayton Award for excellence in teaching in June 2020. In addition to being a teacher, she also has her own tutoring business called "TutoringOutsideTheBox" where she services and tutors elementary students. As a child, Shar'Bral loved to draw, color, and create stories of her own. *Honey's Lost Shoe* is her first children's book, and she plans to create many more. Shar'Bral's vision is to create books for all children to enjoy, learn, and grow. Most importantly, Shar'Bral is passionate about Black and Brown children being physically represented in children's books all around the world.